MUCKY PUP

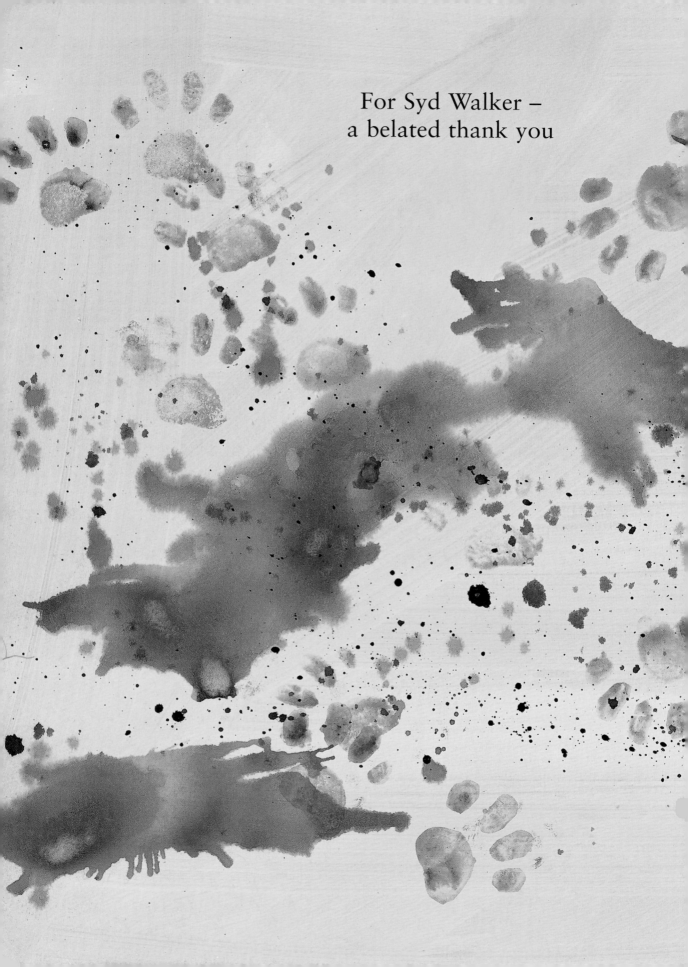

For Syd Walker –
a belated thank you

First published in Great Britain by Andersen Press Ltd in 1997
First published in Picture Lions in 1999
9 10 8
ISBN: 0 00 664656 5
Picture Lions is an imprint of the Children's Division,
part of HarperCollins Publishers Ltd,
77-85 Fulham Palace Road, Hammersmith, London W6 8JB.
Text and illustrations copyright © Ken Brown 1997
The author/illustrator asserts the moral right to be
identified as the author/illustrator of the work.
Printed and bound in Singapore by Imago

First published in Great Britain by Andersen Press Ltd in 1997
First published in Picture Lions in 1999
9 10 8
ISBN: 0 00 664656 5
Picture Lions is an imprint of the Children's Division,
part of HarperCollins Publishers Ltd,
77-85 Fulham Palace Road, Hammersmith, London W6 8JB.
Text and illustrations copyright © Ken Brown 1997
The author/illustrator asserts the moral right to be
identified as the author/illustrator of the work.
Printed and bound in Singapore by Imago

MUCKY PUP

KEN BROWN

PictureLions

An Imprint of HarperCollins*Publishers*

Mucky Pup was having a wonderful time.

He emptied the wastepaper basket,
he cleaned out the coal scuttle,

he rearranged the tablecloth
and shook the cushions.

What fun!

he rearranged the tablecloth
and shook the cushions.

What fun!

The farmer's wife didn't think it was such fun. "Oh, you mucky pup," she cried. "Out you go."

But Mucky Pup wanted to play.
He saw the cockerel.

"Will you play with me?" he asked.

"Cockadoodledon't be stupid," crowed
the cockerel. "I'm a beautiful cockerel –
you're just a mucky pup."

Pup saw the duckling.
"Will you play with me?" he asked.

"You must be quack, quack, quackers,"
quacked the duckling. "I'm a fluffy
duckling – you're just a mucky pup."

Pup saw the cat.

"Will you play with me?" he asked.

"How perrrfectly ridiculous," purred the cat.

"I'm a handsome cat – you're just a mucky pup.

"You must be quack, quack, quackers," quacked the duckling. "I'm a fluffy duckling – you're just a mucky pup."

Pup saw the cat.

"Will you play with me?" he asked.

"How perrrfectly ridiculous," purred the cat.

"I'm a handsome cat – you're just a mucky pup.

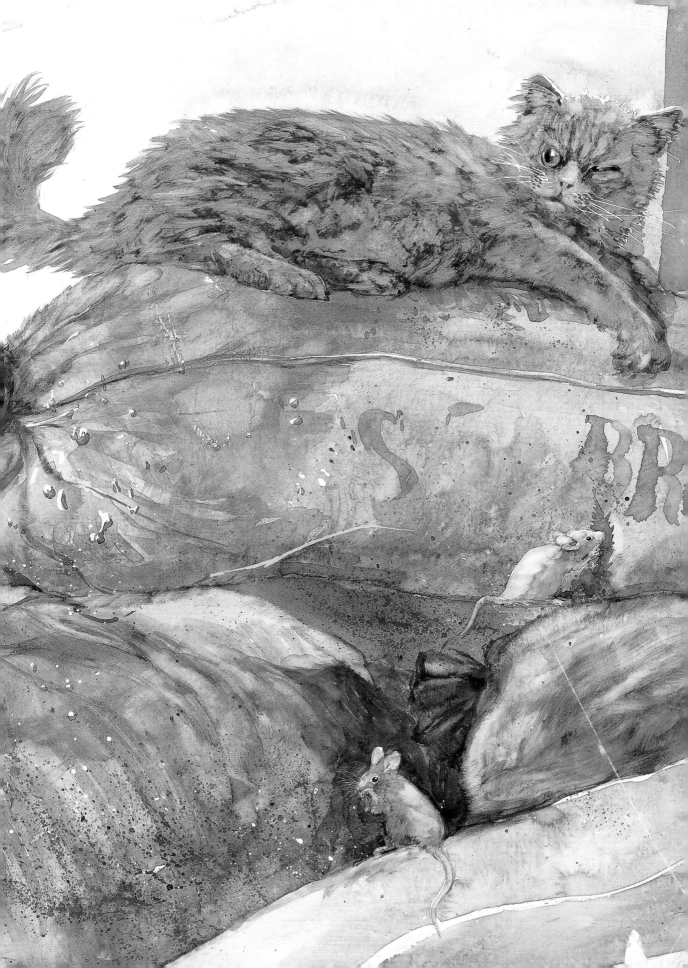

Pup saw the horse.
"Will you play with me, please, please?"
"Nay, nay," neighed the horse. "I'm a
magnificent shire horse – you're just a mucky pup."

Suddenly a
snout appeared
through the bars
of the gate.

"Hello," said the piglet. "Will you play with me?"
"No," said Pup. "I'm just a mucky pup."
"But I'm just a mucky pig," said the piglet.
"Let's play in the mucky mud!"

SPLASH!

He was a good, clean, clever pup,
and he settled down by the fire
to dream about playing
with his mucky piglet
friend tomorrow.